Good-Night, Owl!

PAT HUTCHINS

NIGHT

Simon & Schuster Books for Young Readers

SIMON & SCHUSTER BOOKS FOR YOUNG READERS
An imprint of Simon & Schuster Children's Publishing Division
1230 Avenue of the Americas
New York, New York 10020
Copyright © 1972 by Pat Hutchins
All rights reserved including the right of reproduction
in whole or in part in any form.
Simon & Schuster Books for Young Readers is a trademark of Simon & Schuster
30 29 28
Library of Congress catalog card number: 72-186355
Manufactured in China
ISBN-13: 978-0-02-745900-5 ISBN-10: 0-02-745900-4
0811 SCP

FOR MORGAN'S GRANDPA

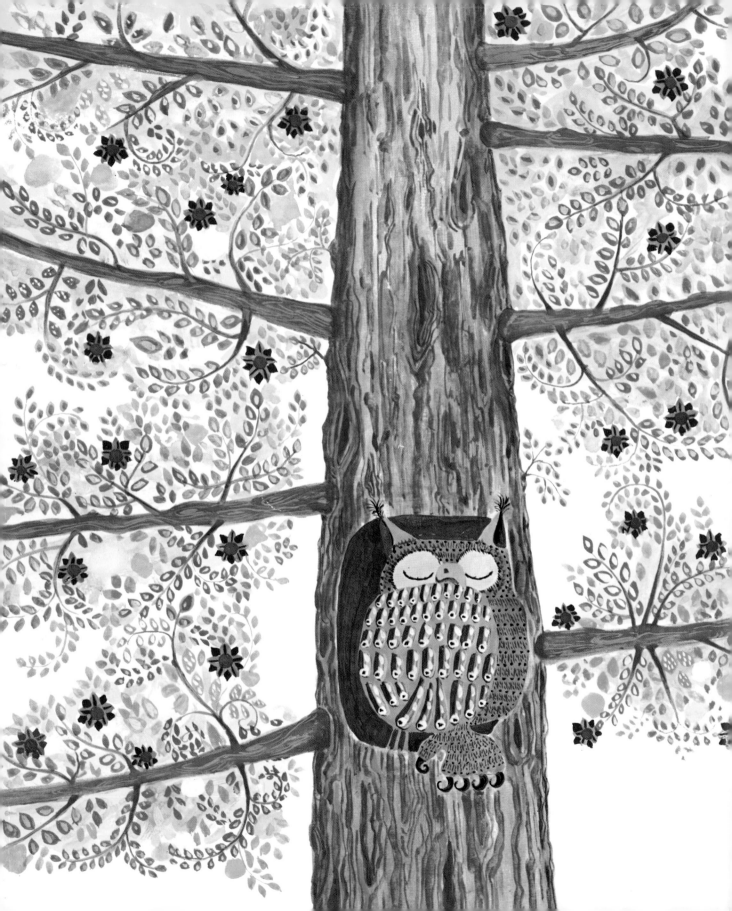

Owl tried to sleep.

The bees buzzed,
buzz buzz,
and Owl tried to sleep.

The squirrel cracked nuts,
crunch crunch,
and Owl tried to sleep.

The crows croaked,
caw caw,
and Owl tried to sleep.

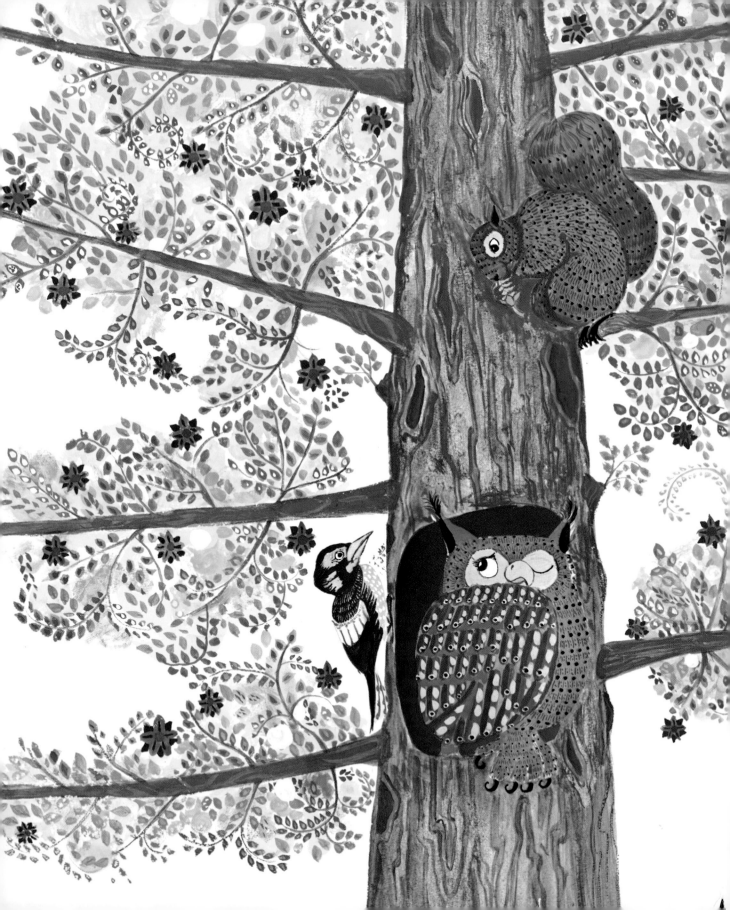

The woodpecker pecked,
rat-a-tat! rat-a-tat!
and Owl tried to sleep.

The starlings chittered,
twit-twit, twit-twit,
and Owl tried to sleep.

The jays screamed,
ark ark,
and Owl tried to sleep.

The cuckoo called,
cuckoo cuckoo,
and Owl tried to sleep.

The robin peeped,
pip pip,
and Owl tried to sleep.

The sparrows chirped,
cheep cheep,
and Owl tried to sleep.

The doves cooed,
croo croo,
and Owl tried to sleep.

The bees buzzed, buzz buzz.
The squirrel cracked nuts,
crunch crunch.
The crows croaked, caw caw
The woodpecker pecked,
rat-a-tat! rat-a-tat!
The starlings chittered,
twit-twit, twit-twit.
The jays screamed, ark ark.
The cuckoo called,
cuckoo cuckoo.
The robin peeped, pip pip.
The sparrows chirped,
cheep cheep.
The doves cooed, croo croo,
and Owl couldn't sleep.

Then darkness fell
and the moon came up.
And there wasn't a sound.

Owl screeched,
screech screech,
and woke everyone up.